www.FlowerpotPress.com
CHC-0909-0480
ISBN: 978-1-4867-1657-9
Made in China/Fabriqué en Chine

Honk, Honk, Vroom, Vroom

Sounds from the City

Written by Jennifer Shand
Illustrated by Barbara Vagnozzi

Did you hear that?

I hear honk, honk, honk and vroom, vroom, vroom!

They're on the move with lots of **beep**, **beep**, **beep** and **zoom**, **zoom**, **zoom**!

What is that?

It's all the cars beeping and honking as they zoom down the road!

I hear lots of **hustle** and **bustle** and **march, march, march!**

There's a lot of **talk** and **walk**, **walk** and **talk** on the **go, go, go**!

What is that?

It's the people hustling and bustling as they walk along the streets!

I hear something backing up with a **beep, beep, beep!**

Then I hear groan, groan, groan and crunch, crunch, crunch!

What is that?

It's a garbage truck picking up trash with a groan and a crunch!

I hear
click-clack, click-clack, click-clack

with a **screech**,
screech,
screech and a
squeal, **squeal**,
squeal!

What is that?

It's the clickety-clack of the subway screeching along the track!

I hear a **grumble, grumble, grumble** and a **growl, growl, growl!**

It's coming to a stop with a **shriek**, **shriek**, **shriek** and a **hiss**, **hiss**, **hiss**!

What is that?

It's a bus shrieking and hissing as it comes to a stop!

I hear ruff, ruff, ruff and bark, bark, bark

with lots of **sniff**, **sniff**, **sniff** and **wag**, **wag**, **wag**!

What is that?

It's the dogs sniffing and wagging all around the dog park!

I hear honk,
honk, hustle,
bustle
and beep,
beep, beep!

I hear click-clack, hiss, hiss and ruff, ruff, ruff!

What is that?

It's all the sounds from the city on a busy day!

Wait...
Did you hear that?